Hi! I'm Robin, Batman's sidekick.

I'm here to tell you what it's like to go through the toughest, trickiest, and most action-packed training in the world: Batman's super hero training.

Remember, the information I am about to share is top secret, and it is forbidden for trainees to try any of these stunts without supervision.

This is the story of how I finally passed Batman's super hero test.

The night began at Arkham Asylum, where Gotham City's biggest bad guys are locked up.

I was helping Batman and Green Arrow stop a jailbreak. The Penguin and Mr. Freeze were trying to spring a bunch of lower-level villains. We had them surrounded when Green Arrow turned toward me.

"Kid, duck!" Green Arrow said, drawing his bow.

BATMAN AND ROBIN'S TRAINING DAY

Adapted by R. J. Cregg
Illustrated by Patrick Spaziante
Batman created by Bob Kane with Bill Finger

Simon Spotlight
New York London Toronto Sydney New Delhi

Based on the screenplay by Heath Corson

Copyright © 2017 DC Comics.

BATMAN and all related characters and elements © ™ DC Comics and Warner Bros. Entertainment Inc. (s17)

SIMON SPOTLIGHT
An imprint of Simon & Schuster Children's Publishing Division
1230 Avenue of the Americas, New York, New York 10020
This Simon Spotlight paperback edition May 2017

For information about special discounts for bulk purchases, please contact Simon & Schuster Special Sales at
1-866-506-1949 or business@simonandschuster.com.
Manufactured in the United States of America 0417 LAK
10 9 8 7 6 5 4 3 2 1
ISBN 978-1-4814-9630-8
ISBN 978-1-4814-9631-5 (eBook)

I didn't listen. Instead, I turned around and saw Commissioner Gordon standing behind me. "How did you get here so fast, Commissioner?" I asked.

"Robin, get down!" Batman commanded.

Finally I ducked, and Green Arrow shot his arrow directly at the good officer.

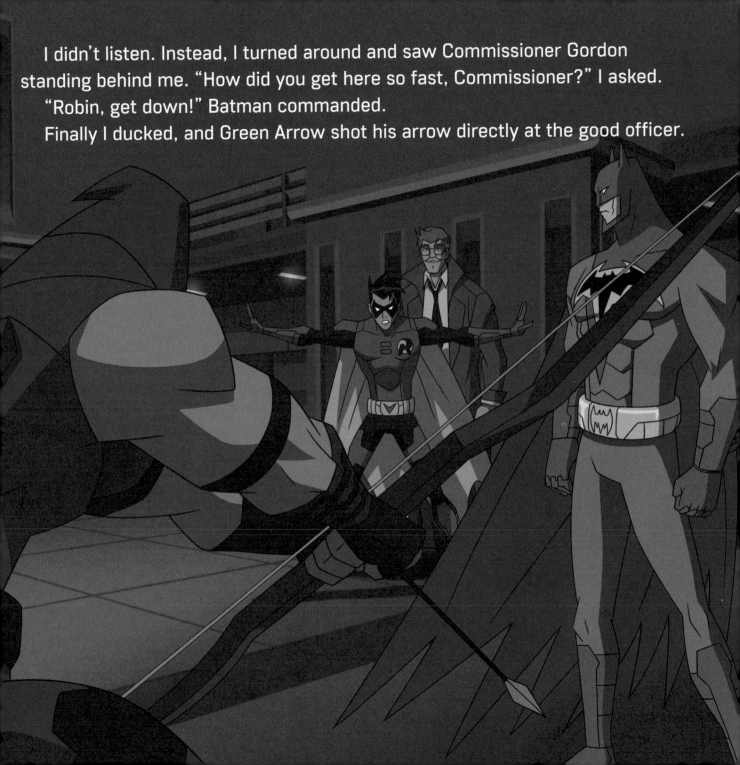

To my surprise the Commissioner transformed into a mountain of clay and the arrow whizzed harmlessly through him. I had been tricked by the shape-shifting villain, Clayface! He pushed me down and used the distraction to escape with his buddies.

"It's okay, kid. You're training with him," Green Arrow said, pointing toward Batman. "That's like diving off the deep end . . . of the ocean!"

Back at the Batcave, I was anxious to clean up the mess I had made.

"The key to catching the bad guys is outsmarting them," Batman said.

I knew Mr. Freeze was a scientist, and the escapees had strange mutations that gave them amazing powers. "Mr. Freeze is using the villains for some kind of experiment!" I said. "And the Penguin must be the mastermind!"

"Good work," Batman said.

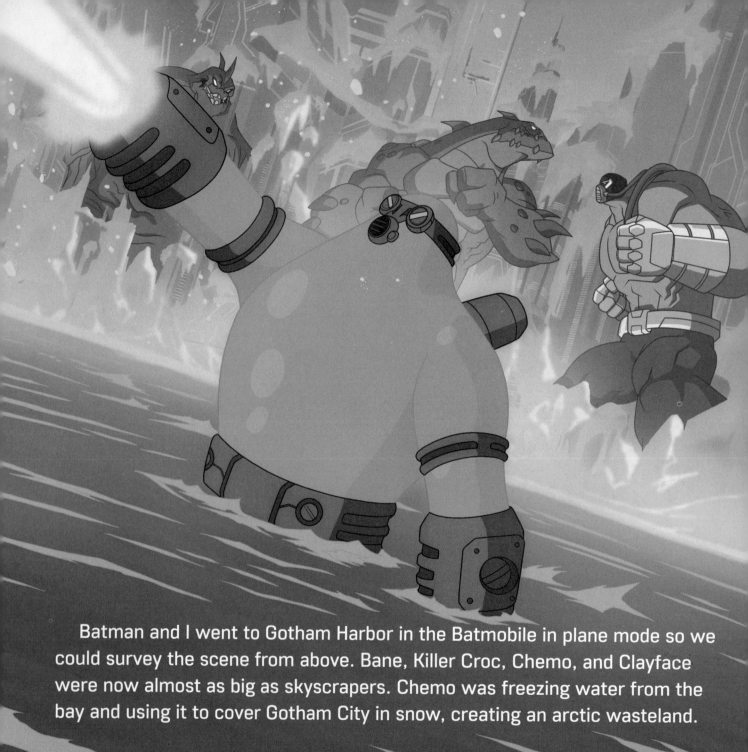

Batman and I went to Gotham Harbor in the Batmobile in plane mode so we could survey the scene from above. Bane, Killer Croc, Chemo, and Clayface were now almost as big as skyscrapers. Chemo was freezing water from the bay and using it to cover Gotham City in snow, creating an arctic wasteland.

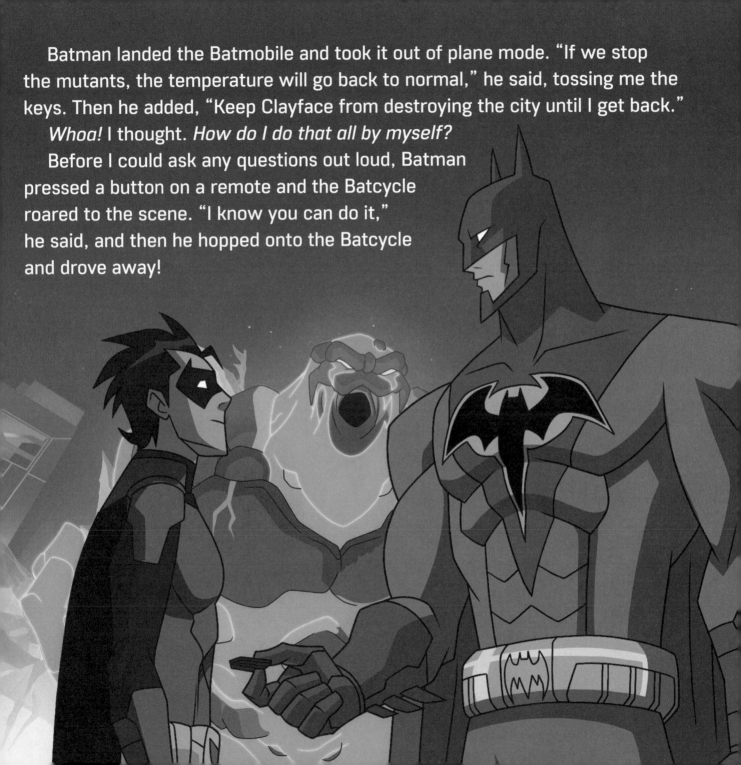

Batman landed the Batmobile and took it out of plane mode. "If we stop the mutants, the temperature will go back to normal," he said, tossing me the keys. Then he added, "Keep Clayface from destroying the city until I get back."

Whoa! I thought. *How do I do that all by myself?*

Before I could ask any questions out loud, Batman pressed a button on a remote and the Batcycle roared to the scene. "I know you can do it," he said, and then he hopped onto the Batcycle and drove away!

So *this* was what Green Arrow meant about training with Batman being like diving into the deep end of the ocean! I was only a beginner, and Batman had left me alone with giant-size Clayface! I wasn't about to let the boss down.

I jumped into the Batmobile. Once I found the ignition, I revved the engine and stepped on the gas. *Man, this thing is fast!* I thought.

Too fast! Soon I was racing straight toward a skyscraper. I knew I couldn't stop the Batmobile on the slippery ice. *How does Batman initiate plane mode?* I thought.

"Uh, plane mode now!" I said out loud.

Whoosh! The Batmobile extended its wings and soared up the side of the skyscraper.

Clayface spewed burning globs of lava in every direction. I had to weaken him. *What does this do?* I wondered and hit a big red button on the Batmobile console.

Blam, blam, blam! The Batmobile fired a barrage of rockets.

"Eat missiles, Lava Breath!" I said as the rockets exploded in Clayface's gooey core. He gushed lava and started to melt down. I thought I had him beat!

Then Clayface used his shape-shifting abilities to pull himself together again.
"I've got you, Boy Wonder!" Clayface boomed at me. With one blow of his
fist, he knocked me out of the sky.

I switched the Batmobile back into car mode, turning what could have
been a crash landing into a fast landing. Even so, I realized I needed help to stop
Clayface!

That's when I heard the roar of the rocket blasters on the Bat-Mech and Green Arrow Mech! My fellow heroes had brought out their biggest robotic suits!

Green Arrow launched his rockets over the bay. "Let's see what you've got, big guy!" he said to Chemo through the mech's loudspeaker.

"I'll take Bane and Croc," Batman said through his comm. He began to fight two mutants at once!

In this epic battle I had to take out Clayface. I wished I had my own mech suit!

Thankfully, Batman sent his friend Dr. Langstrom to help me. "I have plans for a super laser that could theoretically freeze Clayface in his tracks," he said.

I agreed that this was our best chance at stopping Clayface. "Let's construct it on a nearby roof so we have a clear shot at Lava Breath," I said.

We didn't have long to work before Clayface noticed what we were building. "I'll break your silly little laser," he said, coming toward us.

"Incoming!" I warned Dr. Langstrom.

"I need more time!" Dr. Langstrom replied. The laser hadn't been tested, but Clayface reared back his giant fist, ready to break the laser!

"Fire!" I yelled.

Dr. Langstrom blasted Clayface with an icy ray. Flaming globs of lava exploded out of Clayface as he fought back, but the laser was working!

"Just a few more moments and we'll have him fully encased!"
Dr. Langstrom said.

Finally, the last inches of Clayface froze over, and the mega hothead became a mega ice pop.

"Talk about brain freeze!" I quipped, with my heart still racing, but inside I was relieved. *That was close!* I thought.

Batman and Green Arrow brought in the rest of the bad guys. "They'll be fine once they wake up in a cell in Arkham Asylum," said the real Commissioner Gordon.

"Perhaps in confinement, I might find peace," said Mr. Freeze.

The Penguin was less cooperative. "I'll get free, and then I'll have the last laugh over all of you!" he squawked.

The Gotham City Police began melting Clayface down to apprehend him. "That's my cue to leave!" Green Arrow said to the boss. "I'll see you next time, kid," he saluted me as he took off into the night.

I may not have defeated a villain on my own, but I had made Batman proud.

"Robin, I owe you. The whole city owes you," Batman said. "We couldn't have done it without your help today."

Now that you know what it takes to pass Batman's training, what do you think? Could you handle tricky villains, molten monsters, and the most high-tech gear imaginable?

I hope so, because Batman just sent an alert. There's trouble in Gotham City, and he needs our help. Suit up, trainee. It's time to defeat some bad guys!

That meant a lot coming from the big guy, and even though he didn't say it, I knew I earned my spot on the team.